Celebrity ?uiz-o-rama™
SCREEN SCENE
Movie & TV Trivia, Star Scrambles, and Other Games!

Celebrity Quiz-o-rama™

Celebrity ?uiz-o-rama™
SCREEN SCENE
Movie & TV Trivia, Star Scrambles, and Other Games!

by Jo Hurley

SCHOLASTIC INC.

New York   Toronto   London   Auckland   Sydney   Mexico City   New Delhi   Hong Kong

TABLE OF CONTENTS

INTRODUCTION
Take One!

Welcome to Screen Scene, U.S.A.!
Are you ready to flex your pop quiz muscles? How much do you know about who's hot and who's not? When you think of super "stars," what pops into *your* mind first: Freddie Prinze Jr. or your favorite constellation? (Uh . . . if you named *any* star from outer space instead of from Hollywood, you might want to turn back now. . . .)

This is a cool collection of games, puzzles, and trivia quizzes. It gives you a chance to show off how much random information you know about your favorite hunks, sweeties, and 'toons from movies, TV, videos, and books.

Who slays bad guys: Buffy, Brandy, or Britney? Buffy is the best!

What do Amanda Bynes and SpongeBob Squarepants have in common? They both hang with dancing lobsters!

? ? ? **Celebrity Quiz-o-rama**™ ? ? ?

What troublemaking TV star has a saxophone-playing sister? D'oh! It's Bart Simpson, of course!

In addition to multiple-choice quizzes, you'll find super word searches, fill-ins, and code games! The more puzzles you complete . . . the more Pop Points you get! All the answers, plus a positively perfect-o pop scorecard are at the end of the book. You can tally your totals 1-2-3 and see if *you're* top of the pops! But don't peek until you're done.

Is your brain poppin' yet? Screen Scene . . . TAKE ONE!

Throughout the book you can keep track of your Pop Points score — and tally them up as you go.

Let's start off at ground zero for now. . . .

Pop Point Total ___0___

Puzzle 1

Cartoon Survivor

Puzzle Value: 50 Pop Points — whew!

(That's two points for every question you answer correctly.)

Dive right in — for major Pop Points!

You're stranded on a desert island with no hope of escape *unless* you can outsmart the other landlubbers who are stuck there, too. Who are your kooky co-castaways? Why, cartoon characters, of course!

Your only hope at becoming the sole survivor on the island — and sending those other stick figures back to sea — is to put your animation IQ to the test. If you know more about them than they think you do . . . you win!

Ace all 25 answers . . . or be washed up *for good*.

? ? ? Celebrity Quiz-o-rama™ ? ? ?

1. Fred and Wilma's daughter has this Stone Age name.
a) Bam Bam
b) Dino
c) Pebbles

2. What giant cartoon movie featured the voice of Jennifer Aniston as Mom, Annie Hughes?
a) *The Iron Giant*
b) *The Jolly Green Giant*
c) *Beauty and the Giant*

3. In the TV show *Doug*, what's Doug's hilarious last name?
a) Funnie
b) Laughalot
c) Chuckles

4. What happens when a Black Gear is inside a Digimon?
a) It runs faster and twirls around.
b) It turns into an evil Digimon.
c) It turns into a kind creature.

Puzzle 1

5.   What is TV 'toon genius Dexter's favorite school subject?
   a)   Math
   b)   Lunch
   c)   Science

6.   What cartoon bird thinks he sees a "puddy-tat" named Sylvester?
   a)   Stimpy
   b)   Tweety
   c)   Taz

7.   Which character is *not* in Disney's *Beauty and the Beast*?
   a)   Gaston
   b)   Featherduster
   c)   Simba

8.   What animal is Emperor Kuzco turned into in *The Emperor's New Groove*?
   a)   Zebra
   b)   Llama
   c)   Monkey

9. Who does Josie sing with?
a) The Pussycats
b) The Alleycats
c) The Wildcats

10. Which group of characters does *not* belong on The Simpsons?
a) Groundskeeper Willy, Smithers, and Mr. Burns
b) Blossom, Professor Utonium, and Mojo Jojo
c) Apu, Chief Wiggums, and Krusty the Clown

11. Which cute cartoon frog comes from Donut Pond?
a) Pekkle
b) Pikachu
c) Keroppi

12. What kind of animal is Eeyore?
a) Rabbit
b) Kangaroo
c) Donkey

Puzzle 1

13. Where do the Jetsons live?
a) Outer space
b) New York City
c) The jungle

14. Who's the villain in *101 Dalmations*?
a) Natasha Fatale
b) Cruella De Vil
c) Ursula

15. If Snow White is walking along with Bashful, Grumpy, Happy, Doc, and Sneezy, which two dwarfs are missing?
a) Dopey and Sleepy
b) Dopey and Goofy
c) Dopey and Jumpy

16. Who is the youngest Simpson family member?
a) Bart
b) Lisa
c) Maggie

17. What happens to Woody in *Toy Story 2*?
a) He falls off his toy horse.
b) He's stolen by a toy collector.
c) He's threatened by a spaceman toy.

7

18. **What animated movie features Jane Porter and Cheetah as costars?**
   a) *Tarzan*
   b) *The Jungle Book*
   c) *The Lion King*

19. **What do Scooby, Shaggy, Velma, Daphne, and Fred travel around in?**
   a) Magic carpet
   b) Supersonic jet
   c) The Mystery Machine

20. **What's Dil Pickles's *real* first name?**
   a) Dilmore
   b) Dylan
   c) Dilbert

21. **In *A Bug's Life*, what kind of a bug is Flik?**
   a) Grasshopper
   b) Termite
   c) Ant

22. **What kind of animal is Badtz Maru?**
   a) Penguin
   b) Pig
   c) Puppy

Puzzle 1

23. Who's I.R. Baboon's sidekick?

a) I.B. Hyena

b) I.M. Weasel

c) I.M. Llama

24. What kind of pet does SpongeBob Squarepants have?

a) Crab

b) Goldfish

c) Snail

25. Which one is a Powerpuff Girls' rival?

a) Angela Anaconda

b) Space Ghost

c) Princess Morebucks

Pop Point Total _____

Puzzle 2

Name That Star!

Puzzle Value: 5 Pop Points!

Follow the instructions below and cross off some letters. The remaining squares will spell the name of a famous young actor. Hint: He had *The Sixth Sense*.

1. Cross off all your Ps and Qs.
2. Get rid of the letters in columns 3 and 5.
3. Zap away all the letters in the word CURB.
4. X doesn't mark the spot here. Cross it off.

H	X	W	A	D	L	X	E
Y	C	X	J	P	R	O	Q
C	E	Q	P	B	X	L	O
S	U	C	M	P	Q	X	E
R	N	L	U	X	T	B	C

_ _ _ _ _   _ _ _ _

_ _ _ _ _ _

Pop Point Total _____

Puzzle 3

Screening Room

Puzzle Value: 20 Pop Points — or, 1 point for each question you get right

How well do you know what the stars are up to on their shows? Put your Star-Q to the test! Here's the twist: You have to choose the correct *question* for each answer provided. Good luck!

1. Leslie Bibb.
a) Who plays Sam McPherson on *Popular*?
b) Who plays Lily Esposito on *Popular*?
c) Who plays Brooke McQueen on *Popular*?

2. She had superpowers in *The Secret World of Alex Mack* and was a boy-magnet in *10 Things I Hate About You*.
a) Who is Melissa Joan Hart?
b) Who is Larisa Oleynik?
c) Who is Sarah Michelle Gellar?

3. Alyson Hannigan's character on *Buffy the Vampire Slayer*.
a) Who is Willow Rosenberg?
b) Who is Buffy Anne Summers?
c) Who is Cordelia Chase?

4. James Marsden.
a) Who plays Cyclops in *X-Men*?
b) Who plays Superman in *Superman*?
c) Who plays Xena in *Xena: Warrior Princess*?

5. Regis Philbin.
a) Who is the host of *Big Brother*?
b) Who is the host of *Survivor*?
c) Who is the host of *Who Wants to Be a Millionaire*?

6. Jake Lloyd.
a) In *The Phantom Menace,* who plays young Obi-Wan?
b) In *The Phantom Menace,* who plays young Anakin Skywalker?
c) In *The Phantom Menace,* who plays Darth Maul?

Puzzle 3

7. Boy Meets World.
a) What show featured Danielle Fishel as Tabitha?
b) What show featured Danielle Fishel as Topanga?
c) What show featured Danielle Fishel as Tamara?

8. Katie Holmes.
a) Who plays *Dawson's Creek*'s Jen Lindley?
b) Who plays *Dawson's Creek*'s Dawson Leery?
c) Who plays *Dawson's Creek*'s Joey Potter?

9. One million dollars.
a) What is the grand prize on *Big Brother*?
b) What is the grand prize on *Survivor*?
c) What is the grand prize on *Wheel of Fortune*?

10. Jack Dawson.
a) Who was Leonardo DiCaprio's character in *Titanic*?
b) Who was Leonardo DiCaprio's character in *Romeo + Juliet*?
c) Who was Leonardo DiCaprio's character in *Dawson's Creek*?

11. *The Fresh Prince of Bel-Air.*
a) What TV show introduced Will Friedle?
b) What TV show introduced Will Smith?
c) What TV show introduced Wil Horneff?

12. **The actor who plays Chandler Bing on *Friends*.**
a) Who is David Schwimmer?
b) Who is Matthew Perry?
c) Who is Matt LeBlanc?

13. **The name of Dustin Diamond's nerdy character on *Saved By the Bell* and *Saved By the Bell: The New Class.***
a) Who is Scream?
b) Who is Scooter?
c) Who is Screech?

14. **Norwood.**
a) What is *Moesha* star Brandy's real last name?
b) What is *Moesha* star Brandy's last name on the show?
c) What is *Moesha* star Brandy's real first name?

Puzzle 3

15.   Sabrina's aunts on *Sabrina, the Teenage Witch*.

a)   Who are Hildegarde and Zeldegarde?

b)   Who are Hilda and Zelda?

c)   Who are Samantha and Serena?

16.   Robert "Bobby" Boucher Jr.

a)   Who was Adam Sandler's character in *Big Daddy*?

b)   What was Adam Sandler's character in *Little Nicky*?

c)   What was Adam Sandler's character in *The Waterboy*?

17.   The Jackson who plays Pacey on *Dawson's Creek*.

a)   Who is Jeremy?

b)   Who is Jonathan?

c)   Who is Joshua?

18.   Felicity Porter.

a)   What is the role played by Keri Russell on *Felicity*?

b)   What is the role played by Amy Jo Johnson on *Felicity*?

c)   What is the role played by Tangi Miller on *Felicity*?

19. The Grinch.

a) Who was Verne Troyer in *Dr. Seuss' How the Grinch Stole Christmas*?

b) Who was Adam Sandler in *Dr. Seuss' How the Grinch Stole Christmas*?

c) Who was Jim Carrey in *Dr. Seuss' How the Grinch Stole Christmas*?

20. Drew Barrymore's on-screen job as the character of Josie Geller in *Never Been Kissed*.

a) What was a fast-food checkout girl?

b) What was an undercover newspaper reporter?

c) What was a cheerleader?

Pop Point Total _____

Puzzle 4

TV Guy Word Search

Puzzle Value: 15 Pop Points for circling all the TV Guys
10 bonus Pop Points when you ID the mystery TV Guy

Now it's time to seek out the TV guys you love to watch . . . in 3 easy steps!

1. GET SET! Put on your thinking cap, sharpen your pencil, and look over the list.
2. GET CIRCLING! Circle either the FIRST or LAST name in the grid on page 19 — whichever one appears in capital letters on the next page. *The first one is done for you.*
3. GET IT TOGETHER! Write down the *extra*, uncircled puzzle letters to spell the name of *one more mystery guy* and the name of the character he plays on TV.

TV GUY (TV show)

JUSTIN Berfield (*Malcolm in the Middle)*

David BOREANAZ (*Angel*)

NICHOLAS Brendon (*Buffy the Vampire Slayer*)

CARSON Daly (*Total Request Live*)

DAVID Gallagher (*7th Heaven*)

Seth GREEN (*Buffy the Vampire Slayer*)

Joshua JACKSON (*Dawson's Creek*)

BRYCE Johnson (*Popular*)

BUZZ Lightyear (*Buzz Lightyear of Star Command*)*

CHRIS Masterson (*Malcolm in the Middle*)

Tommy PICKLES (*Rugrats*)*

BEN Savage (*Boy Meets World*)

RODNEY Scott (*Young Americans*)

SHAGGY (*Scooby-Doo*)*

BART Simpson (*The Simpsons*)*

BARRY Watson (*7th Heaven*)

*Who says cartoon dudes can't be hunks, too?

Puzzle 4

F	R	A	N	T	R	A	B	K	S
I	J	A	C	K	S	O	N	E	H
D	A	V	I	D	R	M	I	E	A
B	S	N	E	E	R	G	C	C	G
U	O	B	A	R	R	Y	H	A	G
Z	N	N	E	B	R	R	O	R	Y
Z	A	U	N	B	I	I	L	S	N
Z	N	I	T	S	U	J	A	O	A
N	P	I	C	K	L	E	S	N	L
R	O	D	N	E	Y	C	O	L	M

Mystery TV Guy:

_ _ _ _ _ _ _ _   _ _ _ _ _ _

as _ _ _ _ _ _ _ _

19

Puzzle 5

Pop-in-the-Blank

Puzzle Value: 15 Pop Points

Fill-in-the-blanks — *fast*! You can do this puzzle with friends, of course, but it's okay to try it alone, too. Just don't look at the story on page 22 until you first, write the words you need on the chart below. When you're done, turn the page, copy them into the story in order, and laugh out loud (hopefully)!

And Now a Scene From TV...

Favorite TV show _____

Friend who is a girl _____

Friend who is a boy _____

Noisy exclamation _____

Color _____

Kind of pet _____

Puzzle 5

Piece of furniture _____

Liquid _____

Body part _____

Family member _____

Squishy food _____

Hard food _____

Same kind of pet _____

Action word _____

Time of day _____

Your name _____

Number _____

Silly exclamation _____

Wild animal _____

? ? ? **Celebrity Quiz-o-rama**™ ? ? ?

And now a scene from this week's episode of

_____
favorite TV show

Guest starring: _____
friend who is a girl

and _____
friend who is a boy

GIRL: _____! What happened to the
noisy exclamation

_____   _____?
color   kind of pet

BOY: What? It escaped? Did it get out of its

_____ again? Drat!
piece of furniture

GIRL: Look! It left a trail of _____ and
liquid

it seems to have lost its _____
body part

over here on the floor.

BOY: Where's its _____?
family member

Did it escape, too?

GIRL: I knew we shouldn't feed it _____
squishy food

and _____ together.
hard food

22

Puzzle 5

BOY: Let's not worry too much. _____

same kind of pet

only _____ for humans at _____.

action word   time of day

We're safe!

GIRL: But what about _____? I saw

your name

'em _____ minutes ago.

number

BOY: _____! Looks like we may have a

silly exclamation

problem. . . .

GIRL: Next time, we're getting a pet _____

wild animal

instead!

Pop Point Total _____

Puzzle 6

Pop Code

Puzzle Value: 10 Pop Points — one for every right answer

DUH! Somebody at the movie studio got mixed up — and now all the movie titles have coded symbols instead of letters! The bad part: The puzzle looks really weird. The good part: This code can be *cracked*!

To figure out which flick is which, use the code key *and* the movie headline hints to name the ten *lucky* movie titles. . . .

☆	◯	★	✎	❑	✂	✄
A	B	C	D	E	F	G
♦	⌾	↕	♣	✳	◇	✝
H	I	J	K	L	M	N
♥	☞	☛	✤	→	✳	◆
O	P	Q	R	S	T	U
✌	➤	⇨	♠	✒		
V	W	X	Y	Z		

Puzzle 6

1. ✂ ♥ ✏ ⚡ ☞ ✳ ✳ ☆

Headline hint: GROUCHY LIZARD! EGGS HATCHED! CITY CRUSHED!

2. ✳ ☞ ✳ ☆ ✝ ☞ ★

Headline hint: LEO STARS! SHIP SINKS! ICE-BERG BLAMED!

3. ○ ❑ ☆ ♦ ✳ ♠   ☆ ✝ ✏   ✳ ♦ ❑
○ ❑ ☆ → ✳

Headline hint: PRETTY GIRL! UGLY MON-STER! DANCING TEAPOT!

4. ○ ☞ ✂   ✏ ☆ ✏ ✏ ♠

Headline hint: ADAM SANDLER! ORPHAN SON! POP TO IT!

5. ☞ ♥ ♣ ❑ ✧ ♥ ✝   ✳ ♦ ❑
✂ ☞ ♣ → ✳
✧ ♥ ✌ ☞ ❑   ✧ ❑ ▶ ✳ ▶ ♥
→ ✳ ♣ ☞ ♣ ❑ →   ○ ☆ ★ ♣

Headline hint: POKÉ PROBLEMS! ASH COUNTERATTACK!

6. → ✳ ♦ ☆ ✣ ✳   ✳ ☞ ✳ ✳ ✳□

Headline hint: *TEENY MOUSE! NEW FAMILY! KITTY REVENGE!*

7. → ✳ ☆ ✣   ➤ ☆ ✣ →

Headline hint: *RUNAWAY DROIDS! KID-NAPPED PRINCESS! DARTH VADER!*

8. ✳ ♦ □   ➤ ☞ ⤢ ⤢ ☆ ✣ ◖
♥ ✂   ♥ ⤢

Headline hint: *WHICH WITCH? YELLOW BRICKS! GO HOME, DOROTHY!*

9. ✳ ♦ □   ➤ ☞ ⤢ ☆ ✣ ◖   ♥ ✂
♥ ⤢

Headline hint: *GONZO'S GONE! ALIEN INVASION? PUPPET POWER!*

10. ✧ ♦ ☞   ☞ □ ✳ →   ✂ ✣ ♥ ✧
→ ☞ ☆ ★ □

Headline hint: *GIANT ROBOT! OUTER SPACE! PEOPLE SAVED!*

Pop Point Total _____

Puzzle 7

Movie Star Math

Puzzle Value: 10 Pop Points — one per correct answer

How's math class going, guys and gals? Good . . . or *gross*? Well, your number's up with this next pop puzzle! See if you can count on your cartoon, story, and movie-star know-how to tackle these simple math problems.

1. What is the number of kids on *Home Improvement plus* the number of kids who get left alone in *Home Alone plus* the number of lightning bolts on Harry Potter's head?
   a) 5
   b) 4
   c) 3

2. If you invite over Homer and Marge's kids from *The Simpsons*, Tweety, Taz, and Bugs Bunny, how many animated guests will you have?

a) 5

b) 4

c) 6

3. Tommy and Dil Pickles + Angelica Pickles – Chuckie Finster + Susie Carmichaels = how many Rugrats?

a) 4

b) 5

c) 3

4. If the Camden boys (excluding Dad) from *7th Heaven* got together with the Olsen Twins, how many people would be in the room?

a) 2

b) 4

c) 9

5. Number of Powerpuff Girls + the number of heads on CatDog =

a) 4

b) 6

c) 5

6.   Add the number of starring "friends" on *Friends* to the number of kids living at home (not away at military school or anything — hint, hint) on *Malcolm in the Middle* and you get how many?

a) 9

b) 8

c) 10

7.   The sisters from *Party of Five* had lunch with the sisters from *Charmed*. How many girls were hanging out in all?

a) 3

b) 5

c) 4

8.   Air Bud + Salem + Lassie = how many dogs?

a) 0

b) 2

c) 1

9. How many total kids are posing if the stars from *S Club* 7 and *7th Heaven* show up for a group portrait?
   a) 15
   b) 14
   c) 13

10. Scooby-Doo, Shaggy, and Scrappy; Rocky and Bullwinkle; and The Powerpuff Girls are coming over for a BBQ. Zoinks! How many burgers do you throw on the grill (if each guest eats *two*)?
   a) 16
   b) 18
   c) 14

Pop Point Total _____

Puzzle 8

Name That Show

Puzzle Value: 5 Pop Points!

Follow the instructions below and cross off some letters. The remaining squares will spell the name of a popular TV show. Hint: It stars a character who really, *really* likes donuts.

1. You don't need your As, Bs, or Cs.
2. Forget the middle row. Delete it.
3. Cross off each of the corners.
4. You can zap all the letters from V to Z.

S	T	H	A	C	E	Z	D
S	B	I	V	M	X	P	A
Y	A	B	D	L	A	N	R
Z	S	O	C	Y	N	Z	A
S	A	W	A	A	C	S	S

___ _____

Pop Point Total _____

Puzzle 9

In the Nick of Time

Puzzle Value: 20 Pop Points

(It's all or nothing on this one. You've got to get the whole puzzle right to score.)

Now, don't pa-NICK! The NICK mania you are about to encounter is only temporary!

1. Take a NICK-quick look at the clock.
2. Give yourself 15 minutes to use the clues and fill in the following crossword puzzle. Each clue features some fact about a character or show on NICK (Nickelodeon).
3. Try to do it in the NICK of time!

Across
2. Doug Funnie's pet sounds like meat Mom 'n' Dad might make for dinner.
4. How many stages in the final *Double Dare* obstacle course?

32

Puzzle 9

6. What's Angelica's doll's first name?
8. Kenan's pal?
9. He has a "Modern Life."
10. On what show will you see Coach Kreeton and Miss Fingerly?
11. What shape are SpongeBob's pants?
13. Family game show _____ *Dare 2000*
18. Kel's pal?
19. She roams the jungle with Mom and Dad Thornberry and her pet chimp.
21. What do you call a cartoon on NICK?
23. Daggett and Norbert are this kind of ANGRY animal.
24. The name of the wild chimpanzee who belongs to 19 Across.

Down
1. What block of shows features reruns of old TV shows like *The Brady Bunch* and *Head of the Class*? NICK at _____.
2. SpongeBob and Gary live in this yellow fruit that you can also find in Hawaii.
3. Tommy, Dil, and Angelica have this same last name.
5. What body part is CatDog missing that keeps him from wagging along?

6. Which part of CatDog *hates* rock 'n' roll? Cat or Dog?

7. You'd probably say, "HEY!" to this guy with a football-shaped head.

8. What's the name of the place where Sponge-Bob fries up burgers?

10. Her last name is Bynes, and you can see her on *The* _____ *Show*!

12. Tommy's buddy is Chuckie _____.

14. Eddie McDowd needs to perform _____hundred good deeds — *or else*.

15. Last name of the *All That* girl with her own show (hint: rhymes with "lines").

16. Stimpy's sidekick.

17. SpongeBob lives in the undersea city of _____ Bottom.

20. Which "Mack" has a secret world?

22. Doug's girlfriend's name is _____ Mayonnaise.

24. Courage is a cowardly kind of this animal.

Puzzle 9

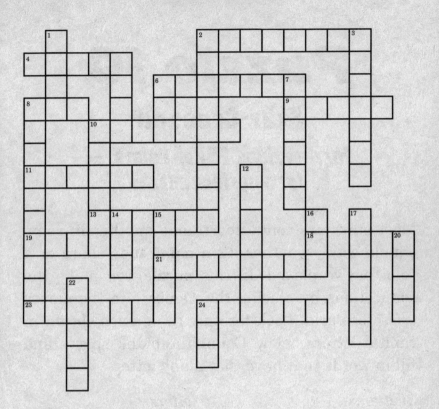

Pop Point Power!

If your name is SpongeBob or Stimpy, you get 50 extra points (and by the way — what were your parents *thinking*?).

Pop Point Total _____

Puzzle 10

Star-Crossed

Puzzle Value: 25 Pop Points — for a perfect puzzle

Most stars are connected to one another in some simple ways, whether it's a name they share or a role they've played. In this puzzle, *you* make the connections by placing the names into the empty crisscross grid. Look for only the names shown in capital letters below. Count the blank spaces and fill in words that have that many letters.

3 letters
BEN Savage
KEL Mitchell

4 letters
Rachael Leigh COOK
Cameron DIAZ
KERR Smith
NEVE Campbell
RYAN Phillippe

5 letters
Seth GREEN
JULIA Stiles
KENAN Thompson
LACEY Chabert
SARAH Michelle Gellar

6 letters
AMANDA Bynes
ANANDA Lewis

Puzzle 10

CARSON Daly
Katie HOLMES
JOSHUA Jackson
Alyssa MILANO

Larisa OLEYNIK
JESSICA Biel

7 letters
Freddie Prinze JR.
Matt LEBLANC
MELISSA Joan Hart

8 letters
David BOREANAZ

9 letters
David GALLAGHER

10 letters
James VAN DER BEEK

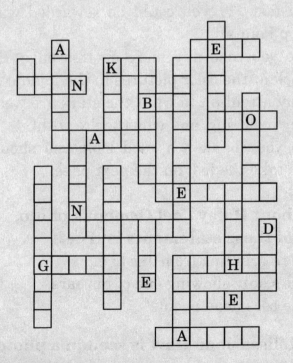

Pop Point Total _____

Puzzle 11

Pop Star Memory Test

Puzzle Value: 20 Pop Points — you know the deal, 2 points for each right answer.

Do you have 20/20 *pop* vision? Cool! If you pass this memory test . . . you could be rewarded with 20 more Pop Points!

Before you read any more on this page, take a quick look at the color pictures in the middle of the book. Pay attention to what the stars are wearing, how they're sitting, and who they're with!

When you've taken a good look, you should be ready to take the test on the next page. . . .

1. About Haley Joel Osment's photo, which of these statements is true?
a) He's grinning from ear to ear.
b) He's only showing one of his ears.
c) He sees dead people!

2. Melissa Joan Hart is seen in a photo with . . .

Puzzle 11

a) Funnyman Jim Carrey
b) Pop princess Britney Spears
c) 'N Sync cutie J. C. Chasez

3. Actress Keri Russell's photo shows her . . .
a) Wearing a hat
b) With long hair
c) With short hair

4. Which *Roswell* characters are shown in their photo?
a) Isabel, Max, Liz, and Michael
b) Maria, Max, Liz, and Alex
c) Isabel, Max, Tess, and Isabel

5. In the Carly Pope and Leslie Bibb photos, which girl is wearing her hair in a braid?
a) Carly
b) Leslie
c) Neither

6. What's Katie Holmes (aka Joey) doing in her photo?
a) Looking sad and pensive
b) Smiling with her fingertip in her mouth
c) Staring straight ahead

7. Which *7th Heaven* star is shown in one of the photos?
- a) Jessica Biel
- b) Barry Watson
- c) David Gallagher

8. Jim Carrey looks like he's doing this in his photo, but he's not.
- a) Standing on his head
- b) Flapping his hands like bird wings
- c) Eating a chili dog

9) Where is Malcolm sitting in his cast photo?
- a) In the middle, of course!
- b) In a convertible
- c) Under a tree

10. In all the color photographs combined — how many guys and how many gals?
- a) 10 guys and 10 gals — everything's equal here!
- b) 13 guys and 8 gals — just because!
- c) Are you crazy? I don't remember that?!

Pop Point Total _____

Puzzle 12

Relativity

Puzzle Value: 15 Pop Points

Everything's relative — especially when it comes to TV and movie stars (even the animated ones!). How good are you at guessing who's related to whom? Give yourself one point for each correct answer.

1.   Brandy and her real-life brother Ray J costar on what hit show?
   a)   *One World*
   b)   *Saved By the Bell: The New Class*
   c)   *Moesha*

2.   The Salinger siblings on *Party of Five* include Bailey, Charlie, Julia, and ...
   a)   Daria
   b)   Claudia
   c)   Angela

41

? ? ? Celebrity Quiz-o-rama™ ? ? ?

3.   Danny Masterson (from *That 70s Show*) has a real-life little brother on TV, too! On what show do you see Chris Masterson?
a)   *Hang Time*
b)   *Malcolm in the Middle*
c)   *Animorphs*

4.   Meredith Monroe and Kerr Smith play which sister-and-brother pair on *Dawson's Creek*?
a)   Joey and Pacey
b)   Bart and Lisa
c)   Andie and Jack

5.   Macaulay Culkin from *Home Alone* has a real-life younger brother who's appeared in movies such as *The Mighty*. What's his first name?
a)   Kieran
b)   Dermot
c)   Scott

6.   What twins appear in their own videos and starred in the TV show *Two of a Kind*?
a)   Randy and Tori Spelling
b)   Mary-Kate and Ashley Olsen
c)   Tia and Tamera Mowry

Puzzle 12

7. This hunk who liked Julia Stiles in *10 Things I Hate About You* went on to play the on-screen son of Mel Gibson in *The Patriot*.

a) Tobey Maguire
b) Heath Ledger
c) Joseph Gordon-Levitt

8. Justin Berfield, Frankie Muniz, and Erik Per Sullivan appear together on *Malcolm in the Middle*. How are they related on TV?

a) Best friends
b) Cousins
c) Brothers

9. What *Friends* brother-and-sister pair are played by David Schwimmer and Courtney Cox Arquette?

a) Ross and Monica
b) Ross and Rachel
c) Ross and Phoebe

10. The Affleck brothers sometimes act together. Their first names are . . .

a) Ben and Matt
b) Casey and Ben
c) Ben and Damon

? ? ? Celebrity Quiz-o-rama™ ? ? ?

11. **Melissa Joan Hart and her sister Emily have both provided voices for characters in what animated series?**
a) *Hey, Arnold!*
b) *Rugrats*
c) *Sabrina, the Teenage Witch*

12. **These real-life brothers grew up on TV! Fred Savage appeared on *The Wonder Years*. On what show did Ben Savage star?**
a) *One World*
b) *Boy Meets World*
c) *Brave New World*

13. **What show features the Camden brothers and sisters?**
a) *The Parkers*
b) *Dawson's Creek*
c) *7th Heaven*

Puzzle 12

14. **This trio of actresses appear as spell-casting sisters on *Charmed*.**
   a) Alyssa Milano, Shannen Doherty, and Jessica Biel
   b) Alyssa Milano, Katie Holmes, and Holly Marie Combs
   c) Alyssa Milano, Shannen Doherty, and Holly Marie Combs

15. **Twin brothers Cole and Dylan Sprouse both acted as one character (Adam Sandler's "son") in *Big Daddy*. What was their character's on-screen nickname?**
   a) Frankenstein
   b) The Waterboy
   c) Little Nicky

Pop Point Total _____

Puzzle 13

Another Pop-in-the-Blank

Puzzle Value: 30 Pop Points
(twice as many as the first — go figure!)

Yeah, yeah. You know the drill. Check out page 20 for instructions. Just don't peek at the story until the words are filled into the chart, superstars!

Got Gossip?

Exclamation _____

Fave movie star (of the opposite gender, please) _____

Same star's name _____

Your name _____

Verb ending in –ing _____

Store you shop at _____

Puzzle 13

Type of food _____

Time of day _____

Funny adjective _____

Sporting event _____

Another verb ending in –ing _____

Name of store _____

Your name (again) _____

Long word _____

Number _____

Descriptive word _____

Noun _____

Faraway place _____

Got Gossip?

_____! Have you heard the latest
      exclamation

gossip about _____?
                      fave movie star

I heard that _____ is seeing _____!
         same star's name   your name

? ? ? Celebrity Quiz-o-rama™ ? ? ?

It's hard to believe, but they were seen together

_____ near _____.
    verb ending in –ing   store you shop at

They stopped for a _____ sandwich
                           type of food

at _____ and then went over to _____
    time of day   funny adjective

Arcade to try a game of _____.
                          sporting event

Later, they were spotted together _____
                       another verb ending in –ing

and shopping at _____. A reliable
                  name of store

source says that _____, now known
                your name

as _____, actually had been tracking
      long word

down this star for _____ years. Reports
                number

are claiming the new pair plan to star together

in an upcoming movie called _____
                    descriptive word

_____ *from Planet* _____.
    noun   faraway place

Pop Point Total _____

Puzzle 14

Happy Birthday!

Puzzle Value: 25 Pop Points — if you can ID more than half of the stars (this is a long one!).

What *famous* peeps share your zodiac sign? Are you ready for a little birthday bonding?

In the following puzzle, you need to fill in the names of superstar birthday boys and girls by using up the BIRTHDAY TILES below. Use the clues to help you identify star names and then plug the right tiles into the blank spaces.

To make it easier to follow, the puzzle is split into the seasons on the calendar. Good luck!

Winter Birthday Tiles
(December, January, and February)

HEW	HOL	EVE	NIF	GAN
ANK	ARR	UNI	STR	CHE
REW	AND	DRE	RYM	

? ? ? Celebrity Quiz-o-rama™ ? ? ?

December
05 FR __ __ __ IE M __ __ __ Z (He's in *"the Mid-dle."*)

11 RIDER __ __ __ ONG (This boy met world, too!)

18 KATIE __ __ __ MES (Her real TV name is Josephine, not Joey.)

January
17 JIM C __ __ __ EY (He's *Ace Ventura* and *the Grinch*.)

22 B __ __ __ RLEY MIT __ __ __ LL (She's *always* in *7th Heaven*.)

29 AN __ __ __ W KEE __ __ __ (He was in *10 Things I Hate About You*.)

February
11 BR __ __ __ Y (She likes a guy named Hakeem on TV.)

21 JEN __ __ __ FER LOVE __ __ __ ITT (She sings *and* acts!)

22 D __ __ __ BAR __ __ __ ORE (Does she live happily *Ever After*?)

Puzzle 14

Spring Birthday Tiles
(March, April, and May)

AMA	MES	NAN	PRI	BOR
LLE	LEY	FRE	MEN	
LLO	HEL	RAH	GEL	

March

05 JAKE __ __ __ YD (Anakin Skywalker . . . is that you?)

08 JA __ __ __ VAN DER BEEK (He's feeling a little "Leery.")

08 __ __ __ DDIE __ __ __ NZE JR. (It's all *Down to You*.)

Same Birthday! Cool!

April

03 __ __ __ NDA BYNES (She's always *All That*!)

10 HA __ __ __ JOEL OS __ __ __ T (Time to *Pay It Forward*.)

14 SA __ __ __ MICHELLE __ __ __ LAR (She'll slay you.)

May

05 DANIE __ __ __ FIS __ __ __ (She thinks Cory Matthews is *fine*.)

10 KE __ __ __ THOMPSON (Usually seen with: Kel.)

16 DAVID __ __ __ EANAZ (You found an *Angel*.)

? ? ? **Celebrity Quiz-o-rama** ? ? ?

Summer Birthday Tiles
(June, July, and August)

ATE	LEE	ASH	MAD
SON	SKI	BEN	MIT
ART	TYL	LEC	ANC

June

10 __ __ __ LEE SOBIE __ __ __ (Felt *Deep Impact* but has *Never Been Kissed*.)

13 MARY-K __ __ __ & __ __ __ LEY OLSEN (Did you know *It Takes Two*?)

22 CAR __ __ __ DALY (He wants your song requests . . . LIVE!)

July

01 LIV __ __ __ ER (Dad sings in rock band Aerosmith.)

21 JOSH H __ __ __ NETT (Too cute for *Here on Earth*.)

25 MATT LE BL __ __ __ (Does he really have any *Friends*?)

August

15 __ __ __ AFF __ __ __ K (Saved the world in *Armageddon*.)

Puzzle 14

16 __ __ __ ONNA (This material girl sings like a
Ray of Light and acts, too!)
25 KEL __ __ __ CHELL (Usually found with:
Kenan.)

Autumn Birthday Tiles
(September, October, and November)

WYN	ONA	SAV	DIC	ROB
ERT	KAT	AEL	PAL	
LON	THA	LIP	CEY	

September

13 BEN __ __ __ AGE (This "Boy" met world a
long time ago. . . .)
28 G __ __ __ ETH __ __ __ TROW (She found
Shakespeare in Love.)
30 LA __ __ __ CHAB __ __ __ (She played violin
on *PO5.*)

October

04 RACH __ __ __ LEIGH COOK (She was in
Huckleberry Finn.)
22 JONA __ __ __ N __ __ __ NICKI (Wanted
Stuart Little to be his brother.)
28 JULIA __ __ __ ERTS (Can anyone catch this
Runaway Bride?)

? ? ? Celebrity Quiz-o-rama™ ? ? ?

November

07 JEREMY AND JASON _ _ _ DON (Twin brothers in real life!)

11 LE _ _ _ RDO _ _ _ APRIO (He couldn't stay afloat in *Titanic*.)

24 _ _ _ HERINE HEIGL (She's seen weird stuff in *Roswell*.)

Pop Point Total _____

Puzzle 15

Star Stuff

Puzzle Value: 30 Pop Points
(This one might be a little tougher so tack on two points for each correct answer!)

Being a star = fame, fortune, and fun! But in many ways, the stars you love are a lot like *you*! They play sports, collect their favorite objects, and have other very interesting hobbies. How much do YOU know about secret star stuff? Test your trivia power right now!

1.   Before he was caught by Buffy, this star of *Angel* played the field — his high school football field, that is.
   a)   Scott Wolf
   b)   David Boreanaz
   c)   Seth Green

? ? ? Celebrity Quiz-o-rama™ ? ? ?

2. Beverley Mitchell says she collects duffel bags — and has 'em stuffed under her bed at home. On what TV show does she appear?
a) *Charmed*
b) *7th Heaven*
c) *Roswell*

3. When she's not hitting the books, this cartoon cutie likes to play the saxophone.
a) Susie Carmichaels
b) Buttercup
c) Lisa Simpson

4. This star wasn't feeling too *Popular* when he cleaned golf balls during one high school summer. (Hint: also known to TV viewers as Josh Ford.)
a) James Marsden
b) Frankie Muniz
c) Bryce Johnson

5. Drew Barrymore thinks these flying creatures are to die for! She has a huge collection of objects shaped like them.
a) Bats
b) Beetles
c) Butterflies

6.   Sarah Michelle Gellar's experience doing this in high school *definitely* helps her on *Buffy*.
a)   Playing on the tennis team
b)   Working in the cafeteria
c)   Taking tae kwon do

7.   Real-life Dawson, actor James Van Der Beek, was a true champion in his childhood. Which one?
a)   He was Little League Champ.
b)   He was King of the Playground.
c)   He was Master of the Universe.

8.   When he's not starring on *7th Heaven*, this actor likes to scuba dive!
a)   Justin Berfield
b)   Ashton Kutcher
c)   Barry Watson

9.   She started as a model, and mountain bikes in her spare time, but who does superstar Jessica Biel play on TV?
a)   Mary Camden
b)   Liz Parker
c)   Joey Potter

? ? ? Celebrity Quiz-o-rama™ ? ? ?

10. This *Roswell* actor has interesting taste buds! He says his fave foods are a toss-up between Fruity Pebbles and sushi. Yecccch!
- a) Brendan Fehr
- b) Wes Bentley
- c) Jason Behr

11. You won't want to "meat" real-life actress Natalie Portman, who plays Princess Amidala in *The Phantom Menace.* Why?
- a) Jar-Jar Binks says she's too busy fighting space villains.
- b) She's a vegetarian.
- c) She rustles cattle in her spare time.

12. This TV teenage witch says Drew Barrymore taught her how to swim!
- a) Melissa Joan Hart
- b) Katherine Heigl
- c) Majandro Delfino

Check out the answers in the answer key.

This young actor received an Academy Award nomination for what movie?

What character did funny man Jim Carrey play in his latest holiday movie?

JC Chasez and Melissa Joan Hart — are they dating?

True or False
Felicity's Keri Russell used to be in TV's
The New Mickey Mouse Club?

What condiment do the "aliens" on
Roswell really like a *lot?*

Carly Pope of *Popular* is from
a) Venezuela b) Vancouver c) Virginia

Leslie Bibb of *Popular* is from
a) Venezuela b) Vancouver c) Virginia

On *Dawson's Creek*, what is Pacey's last name?

With which famous fictional character does Katie Holmes' Joey share the same last name?

He's Simon on *7th Heaven.* His TV pet's name is:
a) Harmony b) Harvey c) Happy

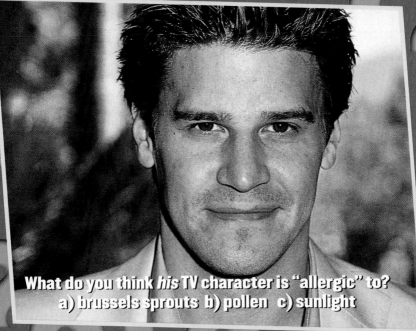

What do you think *his* TV character is "allergic" to?
a) brussels sprouts b) pollen c) sunlight

What's the last name of this TV family?
a) Boomer b) Malcom c) Barbo
d) Trick question: It's never been revealed

Puzzle 15

13. Carson Daly likes to eat Slim Jims and play lots of golf, golf, golf when he's not hosting what hugely popular TV show?
a) *Say What? Karaoke*
b) *Who Wants to Be a Millionaire?*
c) *Total Request Live*

14. Jennifer Love Hewitt keeps her collection of these heavenly items in her bedroom.
a) Cotton balls
b) Angel figurines
c) Model airplanes

15. This *Buffy* regular plays Riley Finn on TV, but he used to play professional basketball in England.
a) Joshua Jackson
b) Marc Blucas
c) Topher Grace

Pop Point Total _____

Puzzle 16

Name That School

Puzzle Value: 5 Pop Points!

Follow the instructions below and cross off some letters. The remaining squares will spell the name of a school where some of your favorite TV characters play and learn! Hint: Where do Powerpuffs practice their ABCs?

1. Get off to a good start. Cross out the second row.
2. Do U know what to get rid of next? Yup! The letter U.
3. Top and bottom squares in the *even* columns need to be zapped.
4. You deserve an A for effort! So let's take away a bad grade: the letter F.

Puzzle 16

P	F	O	S	K	T	E	F
N	R	U	A	K	F	Y	L
U	Y	O	A	K	S	K	U
I	N	F	D	E	R	G	A
R	G	T	Y	E	O	N	Y

_ _ _ _ _ _   _ _ _ _

_ _ _ _ _ _ _ _ _ _ _ _ _ _

Pop Point Total _____

Puzzle 17

Girls Only!

Puzzle Value: 10 Pop Points
(and take 1 extra point if you're a girl!)

Ready for a little girl talk?

Below is a list of real-life actresses and their characters from TV. The only problem is that the names are all scrambled! Can you unscramble them? Hint: Some of the matches have been revealed in other puzzles in this book.

1. Neve Campbell as AIULJ IGRNESLA on *Party of Five*
2. Melissa Joan Hart as RIAASBN NELSPMAL on *Sabrina the Teenage Witch*
3. Carly Pope as MSA CMSPEHRNO on *Popular*
4. Michelle Williams as NJE DIYLENL on *Dawson's Creek*
5. Jennifer Aniston as LAHREC EENGR on *Friends*

6. Danielle Fishel as GNTOAAP ELCWARNE on *Boy Meets World*
7. Taylor Momson as YNIDC ULO HWO in *Dr. Seuss' How the Grinch Stole Christmas*
8. Sarah Michelle Gellar as UYFBF MRESUSM on *Buffy the Vampire Slayer*
9. Beverley Mitchell as YLCU NEDCAM on *7th Heaven*
10. Alyssa Milano as HOBEEP LHLAILEWL on *Charmed*

Pop Point Total _____

Puzzle 18

TV Geography

Puzzle Value: 15 Pop Points

(Give yourself one point for each question you answer correctly.)

Where, oh where, have those TV stars gone?

Oh where, oh where can they be? Hmmmmm . . .

TV geography is totally key when you're getting close to your fave hit-makers. Can you put these questions on the map?

1. All six *Friends* spend their afternoons drinking coffee, gabbing, and hanging out at this New York café. Where?
a) The Coffee Stop
b) Central Perk
c) Lotta Latte

Puzzle 18

2. Where are you most likely to find Eliza Thorn-berry?
a) The jungle
b) At boarding school
c) Underwater

3. Brandy is attending which made-up state university?
a) Arizona State
b) California State
c) New York State

4. In what city does *TRL*'s Carson Daly count down the ten top videos week after week on MTV?
a) Los Angeles
b) Jersey City
c) New York

5. SpongeBob Squarepants lives in an underwater place called:
a) Noodle Kidoodle
b) Bikini Bottom
c) Krusty Krabville

6.   What town do Buffy and her friends keep the monsters away from?
a)   Sunnydale
b)   Sillydale
c)   Monstervale

7.   Where do the *Animorphs* live?
a)   Outer space
b)   In the Yeerk pool
c)   They can't tell you where they live.

8.   Sabrina goes to which high school?
a)   Eastbridge
b)   Northbridge
c)   Westbridge

9.   You'll find Dawson, Pacey, and the rest of the gang in what waterfront town?
a)   Capeside
b)   Seaside
c)   Creekside

10.   Where do Digimons live?
a)   Pokémonland
b)   Digiworld
c)   Dig It Land!

Puzzle 18

11. What was the zip code of the hot show that starred Jennie Garth and Tori Spelling? *Beverly Hills* _____ .

a) 90219
b) 90210
c) 91201

12. Powerpuff Girls Buttercup, Blossom, and Bubbles live in a city called . . .

a) Crimeville
b) Terrorville
c) Townsville

13. Those crazy Flintstones Fred and Wilma have lived in this Stone Age town for a long time.

a) Rockywood
b) Bedrock
c) Rockville

14. On the TV show *Roswell*, the kids are living in what Southwest state where alien spacecraft are supposed to have landed?

a) New Mexico
b) Mexico
c) Arizona

15. Don't have a cow, man! Big shot Bart Simpson goes to this school (just up the road from the nuclear power plant where Dad works, of course!).

   a) Sprainer Elementary
   b) Bean Sprout Elementary
   c) Springfield Elementary

Pop Point Total _____

Puzzle 19

Who Wants to Be a Movie Star?

Puzzle Value: 100 Pop Points for being the star you ARE!

Are you silly or serious? A dancing machine or a wallflower? What would you do if you were stranded on a desert island? Are you a mover, a shaker, or a take-a-break-er? What sort of superstar are YOU most like? Find out!

1. **You've got a GIANT test coming up at school. You:**
a) POWER study! Time to hit the books with some kickboxing moves!
b) Meet your pals at the library for a gossip/studying session.
c) Lock yourself in your room until you know everything.
d) What me, study? Yeah, whatever.

2. These are the kinds of accessories you'd find in your closet:

a) Leather pants, boots, and some serious shades.

b) Faded jeans and Skechers.

c) Reading glasses and color-coordinated slide rules.

d) Baseball cap and bubble gum.

3. You'd find this inside your lunch box:

a) Freeze pops and black licorice.

b) Fresh fruit and cookies.

c) A bologna sandwich.

d) Chocolate milk and bubble gum.

4. This best describes how you relate to your family:

a) "Just leave me alone!"

b) "Let's have a family picnic this weekend!"

c) "Pick me up at the library, please."

d) No words — just laughter.

Puzzle 19

5. You're crushing on someone in your class. What do you do?

a) Let him or her invite you out. You're too cool to ask first.

b) Grab a burger and a movie? Sure you will!

c) You're too busy studying to date anyone.

d) No words — just laughter.

6. You're flipping through the TV guide and your favorite show is on cable:

a) *Batman*. You love stories of good vs. evil.

b) *The Wizard of Oz*. You love Dorothy and Toto.

c) Reruns of *Bill Nye, the Science Guy*. You love brains.

d) *I Love Lucy* reruns. You love *laughing* best.

7. You drop your tray in the school cafeteria. You're so embarrassed . . .

a) But who cares! You pick up your mess and roll your eyes.

b) You turn three shades of purple. Whoopsie!

c) You crawl under a table and stay there until everyone leaves.

d) You turn it into a joke and blame the kid behind you.

8. Inside your locker, someone would find:

a) Black nail polish, temporary tattoos, and a copy of *The Powerpuff Girls* CD.

b) An *'N Sync* CD, glitter barrettes, and a photo of your BFF.

c) A dictionary, sharpened pencils, and an apple (for your teacher!).

d) A picture of Goofy, Adam Sandler's autograph, and bubble gum.

9. Who wants to be a millionaire? If you won a million dollars you'd:

a) Charter a plane to New York City or Los Angeles so you could hang with *stars*.

b) Fly to Paris or somewhere else really romantic.

c) *Save* your money. You can go anywhere inside a book anyway.

d) What *you*, win a million dollars? Ha-ha!

Puzzle 19

10. Your idea of a true-blue friend is:

a) Someone with whom you can play a practical joke.

b) Someone you'd save from a practical joke.

c) Someone who doesn't believe in practical jokes.

d) Someone on whom you can play a practical joke.

FINAL Pop Point Total _____

ANSWER KEY

Answers to Questions on Back Cover

● The Powerpuff Girls are Blossom, Bubbles, and Buttercup

● Sarah Michelle Gellar plays Buffy

● Haley Joel Osment starred in *The Sixth Sense*

● Yes, there *really* will be a movie of Harry Potter in 2001

Puzzle in the Middle

Here are the answers to the caption-questions on the pictures in the middle of this book.

1. He's Haley Joel Osment; the movie is *The Sixth Sense.*
2. The Grinch, in *Dr. Seuss' How the Grinch Stole Christmas.*
3. No! But they *are* friends.
4. True.
5. Tabasco sauce.
6. b) Vancouver.
7. c) Virginia.

ANSWER KEY

8.   Witter.
9.   Potter, Harry.
10. c) Happy.
11. c) Sunlight.
12. d) Trick question!

Puzzle 1: Cartoon Survivor

1. c	6. b	11. c	16. c	21. c
2. a	7. c	12. c	17. b	22. a
3. a	8. b	13. a	18. a	23. b
4. b	9. a	14. b	19. c	24. c
5. c	10. b	15. a	20. b	25. c

Puzzle 2: Name That Star!

H	X	W	A	D	L	X	E
Y	C	X	J	P	R	O	Q
C	E	Q	P	B	X	L	O
S	U	C	M	P	Q	X	E
R	N	L	U	X	T	B	C

Answer: HALEY JOEL OSMENT

? ? ? Celebrity Quiz-o-rama™ ? ? ?

Puzzle 3: Screening Room

1. c	5. c	9. b	13. c	17. c
2. b	6. b	10. a	14. a	18. a
3. a	7. b	11. b	15. b	19. c
4. a	8. c	12. b	16. c	20. b

Puzzle 4: TV Guy Word Search

F	R	A	N	T	R	A	B	K	S
I	J	A	C	K	S	O	N	E	H
D	A	V	I	D	R	M	I	E	A
B	S	N	E	E	R	G	C	C	G
U	O	B	A	R	R	Y	H	A	G
Z	N	N	E	B	R	R	O	R	Y
Z	A	U	N	B	I	I	L	S	N
Z	N	I	T	S	U	J	A	O	A
N	P	I	C	K	L	E	S	N	L
R	O	D	N	E	Y	C	O	L	M

Mystery TV Guy is *FRANKIE MUNIZ as MAL-COLM*

ANSWER KEY

Puzzle 5: Pop-in-the-Blank

Uh, hello? No wrong answers here. Give yourself all the points on the page and move along, will ya?

Puzzle 6: Pop Code

1. *GODZILLA*
2. *TITANIC*
3. *BEAUTY AND THE BEAST*
4. *BIG DADDY*
5. *POKÉMON THE FIRST MOVIE: MEWTWO STRIKES BACK*
6. *STUART LITTLE*
7. *STAR WARS*
8. *THE WIZARD OF OZ*
9. *MUPPETS FROM SPACE*
10. *THE IRON GIANT*

Puzzle 7: Movie Star Math

1. a ($3 + 1 + 1 = 5$
2. c ($3 + 1 + 1 + 1 = 6$)
3. c ($2 + 1 - 1 + 1 = 3$)
4. b ($2 + 2 = 4$)
5. c ($3 + 2 = 5$)
6. a ($6 + 3 = 9$)

??? Celebrity Quiz-o-rama™ ???

7. b (2 + 3 = 5)

8. b (2 — Air Bud and
   Lassie are dogs;
   Salem is a cat)

9. c (7 + 6 = 13)

10. a (3 + 2 + 3 = 8 x 2
    burgers = 16)

Puzzle 8: Name That Show

S	T	H	A	C	E	Z	D
S	B	I	V	M	X	P	A
Y	A	B	D	L	A	N	R
Z	S	O	C	Y	N	Z	A
S	A	W	A	A	C	S	S

Answer: THE SIMPSONS

ANSWER KEY

Puzzle 9: In the NICK of Time

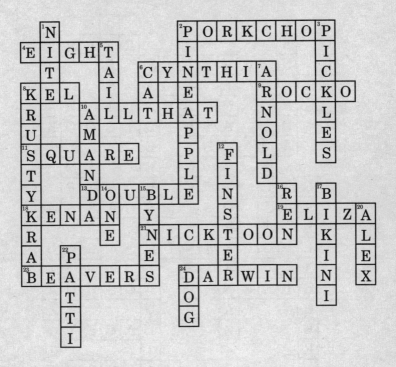

Puzzle 10: Star-Crossed

ANSWER KEY

Puzzle 11:   Pop Star Memory Test

1b; 2c; 3b; 4a; 5c; 6b; 7c; 8b; 9a; 10b or c are both good — take the points and keep on smiling!

Puzzle 12:   Relativity

1. c	6. b	11. c
2. b	7. b	12. b
3. b	8. c	13. c
4. c	9. a	14. c
5. a	10. b	15. a

Puzzle 13:   Another Pop-in-the-Blank

HELLO? Didn't you read the rules the first time around?

No winners. All points. Take 'em and run. . . .

Puzzle 14:   Happy Birthday!

WINTER TILES

December

05	FRANKIE MUNIZ
11	RIDER STRONG
18	KATIE HOLMES

? ? ? Celebrity Quiz-o-rama™ ? ? ?

January

17 JIM CARREY
22 BEVERLEY MITCHELL
29 ANDREW KEEGAN

Febuary

11 BRANDY
21 JENNIFER LOVE HEWITT
22 DREW BARRYMORE

SPRING TILES

March

05 JAKE LLOYD
08 JAMES VAN DER BEEK
08 FREDDIE PRINZE JR.

April

03 AMANDA BYNES
10 HALEY JOEL OSMENT
14 SARAH MICHELLE GELLAR

May

05 DANIELLE FISHEL
10 KENAN THOMPSON
16 DAVID BOREANAZ

ANSWER KEY

SUMMER TILES

June
10 LEELEE SOBIESKI
13 MARY-KATE & ASHLEY OLSEN
22 CARSON DALY

July
01 LIV TYLER
21 JOSH HARTNETT
25 MATT LE BLANC

August
15 BEN AFFLECK
16 MADONNA
25 KEL MITCHELL

AUTUMN TILES

September
13 BEN SAVAGE
28 GWYNETH PALTROW
30 LACEY CHABERT

October
04 RACHAEL LEIGH COOK
22 JONATHAN LIPNICKI
28 JULIA ROBERTS

? ? ? Celebrity Quiz-o-rama™ ? ? ?

November

07   JEREMY AND JASON LONDON
11   LEONARDO DICAPRIO
24   KATHERINE HEIGL

Puzzle 15: Star Stuff

1. b	6. c	11. b
2. b	7. a	12. a
3. c	8. c	13. c
4. c	9. a	14. b
5. c	10. b	15. b

Puzzle 16: Name That School

P	F	O	S	K	T	E	F
N	R	U	A	K	F	Y	L
U	Y	O	A	K	S	K	U
I	N	F	D	E	R	G	A
R	G	T	Y	E	O	N	Y

ANSWER: Pokey Oaks Kindergarten

ANSWER KEY

1. Neve Campbell as JULIA SALINGER on *Party of Five*

2. Melissa Joan Hart as SABRINA SPELL-MAN on *Sabrina, the Teenage Witch*

3. Carly Pope as SAM MCPHERSON on *Popular*

4. Michelle Williams as JEN LINDLEY on *Dawson's Creek*

5. Jennifer Aniston as RACHEL GREEN on *Friends*

6. Danielle Fishel as TOPANGA LAWRENCE on *Boy Meets World*

7. Taylor Momson as CINDY LOU WHO in *Dr. Seuss' How the Grinch Stole Christmas*

8. Sarah Michelle Gellar as BUFFY SUM-MERS on *Buffy the Vampire Slayer*

9. Beverley Mitchell as LUCY CAMDEN on *7th Heaven*

10. Alyssa Milano as PHOEBE HALLIWELL on *Charmed*

Puzzle 18: TV Geography

1. b	6. a	11. b
2. a	7. c	12. c
3. b	8. c	13. b
4. c	9. a	14. a
5. b	10. b	15. c

Puzzle 19: Who Wants to Be a Movie Star?

If You Picked Mostly As: YOU'RE A REBEL and you'd relate best to stars like:
Sarah Michelle Gellar (Buffy) on *Buffy;* Carly Pope (Sam) on *Popular*; David Boreanaz (Angel) on *Angel*; Joshua Jackson (Pacey) on *Dawson's Creek;* Buttercup on *The Powerpuff Girls;* and actress Christina Ricci.

If You Picked Mostly Bs: YOU'RE A NICE GUY (OR GAL) and you'd relate best to stars like:
Katie Holmes (Joey) on *Dawson's Creek;* Beverley Mitchell (Lucy) on *7th Heaven;* actor Freddie Prinze Jr.; Brandy (Moesha) on *Moesha;* Bubbles on *The Powerpuff Girls;* and MTV's *Total Request Live* host Carson Daly.

ANSWER KEY

If You Picked Mostly Cs: YOU'RE A SMARTY-PANTS and you'd relate best to stars like:
>Eliza Thornberry; Lisa Simpson; Ben Savage (Cory) on *Boy Meets World;* actress Natalie Portman; Blossom on *The Powerpuff Girls;* Lacey Chabert (Claudia) on *Party of Five;* and actor Haley Joel Osment.

If You Picked Mostly Ds: YOU'RE A GOOF and you'd relate best to stars like:
>Jim Carrey; Adam Sandler; Amanda Bynes, Kenan, or Kel on *All That*; Lisa Kudrow (Phoebe) on *Friends;* Scooby and Shaggy on *Scooby-Doo;* and Frankie Muniz (Malcolm) on *Malcolm in the Middle.*

Don't forget: no matter *who* you're the most like — you still get 100 points! Hooray!

POP POINT SCORECARD

Rack up Pop Points and see your score! Are you a superstar . . . or *what*?

POP POINT TOTAL   POP RATING

0–49   HOP ON POP

You wanna be the SuperKid of Pop . . . but you're a little out of sync! *Think!* When's the last time you turned on Nick at Nite or 'tooned into a Bugs Bunny rerun? With a little help, you'll be up to speed on your Homer Simpson know-how in "D'oh!" time. Keep it real.

50–149   POP FLY

Not too bad, you l'il pop-start! You know the basics about the best shows and top movies . . . *but* you haven't quite narrowed down who's who. You know Buffy's a slayer — but you can't remember if it's dragons or vampires that she's zapping to dust. That's okay, though. Even a pop fly means you've still got the potential to slam a home run. . . .

? ? ? Celebrity Quiz-o-rama™ ? ? ?

150–249   POP YOUR CORK

Hot diggity! You sure do pop the cork when it comes to your Pop-Q — from *Dawson's Creek* to *Roswell* to Whoville . . . you've got the pop territory *totally* down. Way to go! Now, turn your 'tude onto special stars like SpongeBob Squarepants or Carson Daly — and see what pops up!

250–349   CHERRY POP

You're the pop queen or king of the planet, right? You know Buffy's last name is a season (Summers) and that Doug's friend Patti's last name is a food (Mayonnaise). You know the name of every Digimon and you vote every week on MTV's *Total Request Live*. BUT . . . you don't have pop perfection. Not yet!

350–infinity   MAKE YOUR EYES POP

You're like a pop top — flip you open and you keep on fizzin'. Way to go with the pop stats, smarty! Who knew that memorizing the Powerpuffs' theme song or reading *Nickelodeon* magazine could pop you off the charts? Well, it has. You're the poppiest — and you'd make *anyone's* eyes pop!